FALCON'S MATE

A BIRD-SHIFTER NOVELLA

MICHELLE M. PILLOW

MICHELLEPILLOW.COM

Princess Ari knows it's her time to marry and has picked out several suitable men in her mind—none of which are Falcoan Army Commander, Rurik of the Fifth. Who cares if he's sexy and all the women want him? The man tormented her when they were children, causing her untold humiliations. Luckily, there is really no need to worry about such a match. Shifters cannot rule and Rurik is a natural born falcon shifter. But it would seem fate has other ideas.

This book was first published in "Talons", a multi-author print anthology, and in a matching ebook collection as "Talons: Seize the Hunter".

Fun Fact: Falcon's Mate takes place in the Qurilixen Universe!

Dragon Lords Series
Barbarian Prince
Perfect Prince
Dark Prince
Warrior Prince
His Highness The Duke
The Stubborn Lord
The Reluctant Lord
The Impatient Lord

The Dragon's Queen

Lords of the Var® Series
The Savage King
The Playful Prince
The Bound Prince
The Rogue Prince
The Pirate Prince

Captured by a Dragon-Shifter Series
Determined Prince
Rebellious Prince
Stranded with the Cajun
Hunted by the Dragon
Mischievous Prince
Headstrong Prince

Space Lords Series
His Frost Maiden

His Fire Maiden
His Metal Maiden
His Earth Maiden
His Woodland Maiden

Dynasty Lords Series
Seduction of the Phoenix
Temptation of the Butterfly

To learn more about the Qurilixen World series of
books and to stay up to date on the latest book list
visit www.MichellePillow.com

AUTHOR UPDATES

To stay informed about when a new book is released sign up for updates:

michellepillow.com/author-updates

To my fans. Thank you for your constant support.

PLANET FALCONIA

PRINCESS ARI DISLIKED the warriors who flew in the Falcoan Army, but none punctured her thoughts like Commander Rurik of the Fifth. She hated him and his smug, self-confident attitude. He'd thought himself so superior when they were children—swooping down to knock her on her ass so her new gown would become covered in muck, or overtaking her in games because of his naturally enhanced stamina and strength—and all because he was born a falcon shifter. His kind was rare and given the utmost consideration, as they were destined to lead the armies that guarded her home planet against outsiders. All other warriors turned after birth, their powers enhanced by choice, not fate. Rurik was a falcon by destiny, and it made him impossibly arrogant to deal with. He'd grown up training at her home in the palace and was constantly around to torment her.

And now he was coming back.

Well, she had news for him. She was no longer the awkward, gangly girl he'd known. She'd gone through puberty late, very late, but her powers had come to her, as they did all non-shifting Falconians. She'd been sixteen seasons, nearly twenty-four years according to the calendar they observed from the Old Way, and her father had begun to worry she'd never bloom. Too bad Rurik had been deployed to his post merely days before it happened. She would've loved to prove him wrong about her.

It didn't matter. Now she was a powerful, envied princess, and soon she'd be queen. With her mother gone, she was the sole female of power on their planet. She controlled the armies. She controlled Rurik. And, with the evening's corona-tion ceremony well upon her, she would control the entire planet. Her father would step aside, for men did not rule as well as women. Falconian males' blood ran too hot.

That is why Rurik was coming back. All commanders were to be in attendance, for tonight was the shifting of power. But first, there was another ceremony—one that took place this very afternoon. Today she would drink from the sacred Chalice and awake next to the man who was to be their future king, her husband, her mate, her eternal lover. And it couldn't come too soon, as far as she was concerned.

Whereas normal women of their society could take as many lovers as they pleased, she was held to a higher standard. Until she married, she was allowed three semi-lovers with whom all pleasures of the flesh were allowed but one—the final claiming of her heart. If things got too close, she was obligated to end it. In a life that kept her in front of the eyes of all, she longed for someone to hold her in the night, to look at her with eyes not judging but seeing. She wanted the comfort and safety of a man who would not leave her.

Her first lover, a traveler and diplomat who visited them soon after her powers had come to her all those years ago, had been to spite Rurik. He'd been an *enfem*, a slender, pale man who spoke and acted as far from a hot-blooded warrior as possible without being an actual woman. She still cursed that wasted pick. Whereas he did hold her, he also cried most of the night speaking of his feelings.

Falconian women were stronger than he was. The second man she thought she could someday love, until she realized that lust and love were two different things. The third was a practical choice, if not her best one. He'd been an older man, a trainer who instructed more than participated.

Ari looked at her reflection in the still water that made up one wall of her bedroom. She could touch the wetness, but magic kept it from caving in on her and soaking her. It was a good thing too. Her hair had taken three skilled hairdressers four hours to do. The waist-length red locks were twisted around strands of wire to keep it in place and then bent around her head to fashion an intricately beautiful crown. It towered above her, five hand spans high in the front and tapered down to a half span in the back.

Her gown was of the finest weave, held into place with a thick metal band that wrapped around her chest and back, leaving her tanned shoulders bare. The band was bent to fit her body perfectly, molding along the top of each breast to keep the flowing material that hung from it from falling down. The royal dark-red material moved with her, clinging and releasing her curves with each step as if it were air.

Holding her arms to the side, she waited as her attendants slipped silver coils onto her arms. They wound around from shoulder to wrist, decorated with the shiny black stones found only in the dark depths of Falconia's lucid waters. A matching stone hung from the chain that dangled from her hair, down the part in the middle of her head.

Black makeup outlined her large blue eyes, made all the more noticeable by a dark-red stripe that stretched from temple to temple, encircled both eyes and crossed over the bridge of her nose. The red matched the color on her lips.

Turning, she looked to the mating bed that had been prepared in the center of the room. The Chalice never chose poorly or with cruel intentions. It was neutral and often its choice led to happiness for both parties. At least, it gave a happy start. What the two people did with the mating given them was up to the couple, and there had been those who ruined a good thing.

Unlike the peasants who could draw a ring in the dirt to form the mating circle, her bed was that of a princess. It was high up on a raised platform, so tall she couldn't see the top of it from her place on the floor. Above it, the water wall curved with the true ceiling, giving her a reflection of thick gold and red pillows encircling the edges and an abundance of silk to lie upon. Sweet herbs were scattered on the floor around it. So strong was the ancient spell, no one could cross the herbs and reach the bed. Only the Chalice's magic could break through the boundary, carrying her and her husband inside. She knew that even if she was inside, none could see her. All they would see was the view she saw now...a reflection of an empty bed.

Inside the herbal sphere, it would be as dark as deep space. The magical boundary around the edge would keep them from falling as she and her mate consummated what was to be. Whether they shared names before was up to them. Some married couples did, others didn't. Ari had decided to let the male's actions guide hers. Clearly, since it was her marriage ceremony, he would know who she was.

"Princess?" Vara, her best friend and head attendant spoke quietly, signifying that they were done, and it was time.

In all, there were ten attendants, all daughters from noble families. Vara was a cousin, as was her younger sister Petra. Should Ari die, Vara would take the throne. Some thought Ari foolish for keeping Vara as a close and trusted friend, but she wasn't scared. Vara would never hurt her. Their bond was too close for that. Besides, Ari knew Vara's deepest secret. She longed to be in the armies, flying into battle. Politics were too tame for her. Someday, Ari hoped to give Vara a chance at her dream, though she hadn't told her cousin as much.

Petra was just a child—the youngest attendant honored because she was family. Maura, Aurelie, Thora, and Lena came from the different providences around the queendom. She knew them from childhood and thought well enough of them to honor them.

Lucia, Adria, Jael, and Clarinda were all from a neighboring castle. Their dark skin was a beautiful brown, enhanced by the prettiness of their big, round, brown and green eyes. Their father, Lord Viceious, was Supreme General to all the armies and a man Ari had dealt with on many occasions. Their being honored as attendants was merely politics. She had no close connection to the four girls.

The women had been unusually quiet, as was tradition, giving her time to contemplate whatever it was she should have been contemplating on this day. Unfortunately, Commander Rurik was the thing that kept popping into her head. She knew it was because she'd heard his name that morning, whispered in girlish excitement. A maid saw him arrive with his men, swooping down from the skies to land within the palace walls.

"I am ready," Ari stated, lifting her chin. With a small wave, she parted the liquid along the water wall, creating an archway. "Join the others in the hall. Vara will walk with me."

The attendants rushed from the room through the new door, leaving Ari alone with Vara.

"You're distracted." Vara threaded her arm through Ari's. Her cousin was a slender woman but had the skill of the best warriors when it came to using a talon glove. With it, she could be deadly. Looks really were deceiving. Vara's purple gaze, wavy brown hair and dark brown complexion were the envy of many women.

"Yea." Ari nodded. "Rurik is here."

"Ah, I remember him. He's the one you gave a blood oath to avenge yourself against." Vara gave a small laugh. "Is that what you're doing on your Mating Day? You're plotting revenge for childish hurts?"

"Childish?" Ari gasped. "You call wanting a

little vengeance for being knocked off a platform into a bed of dung in my coronation dress on the day I was crowned as a princess a small affair? It's permanently recorded in the Book of Ari as historical fact. I can't erase that. Only three moons ago I saw it again when I was flipping through my life."

"Ah, perhaps not."

"Or when he slipped that love note under my pillow, making me believe that Mikael wanted to marry me? I made an ass out of myself in front of the whole palace."

"Mikael is still very sexy. I don't blame you for being mad about that."

"He still looks at me as if I might try and kiss him again," Ari mumbled.

"You did embarrass him by doing it in front of the other flyers," Vara said. She pulled Ari's arm, urging her to walk through the door in the water wall. A long hallway stretched before them, angling toward the ground, leading directly to the hall. Since her chambers were set high above the ground without support from underneath, the door in the great hall was the only way in or out—unless you were a falcon shifter, in which case you could fly up to a window. "Did you ever discover for certain whom the note was from?"

"Nae. I cannot prove it, but I'm sure it was a prank. Rurik is the only man who'd have the nerve to do such a thing. He didn't deny it." Even now, remembering the simple, horribly unpoetic words, she felt a twinge in her heart.

"That's mean," Vara whispered needlessly.

"I'll show Commander Rurik that I am no one to be trifled with." Ari smiled at her cousin. Yea, she would show him, and when the supreme power to rule was hers, she'd make sure he and his legion of men were shipped to the other side of the planet. He would spend his days protecting Falconia's marshes from outside invasions.

Commander Rurik smiled as he entered the palace's great hall in the center eye of the castle. They called it the "center eye" because the castle looked like the stylized shape of an eye when they flew over it. Two curved walls formed the battlements along the outside. Yards and gardens were where the whites would normally be and in the iris was the main palace tower.

It was strange being back in the palace after so many years away. He'd grown up there, as did the other natural born falcon shifters. They had been treated like royalty, given the best education, trained to be lethal warriors and yet held apart by what they were. Being natural born gave them one place in Falconia's society—the life of a commander. Other warriors chose to fly in the armies. The pure bloods were born to do it.

He would be expected to marry a woman with little money and power. His position afforded him any comfort, and it would honor his name to elevate a woman who had little, and help to support her family, but he wasn't allowed to marry a nobleman's daughter—not with his bloodline. He never fully understood how he could be so revered, so trusted to protect lives, and yet so undesired as a son because of his falcon birth. Honor kept the commanders from rebelling, and they never thought of taking over the planet, though they easily could.

The pure falcons had ruled before, and they'd nearly lost the planet due to their rash actions. After, it became acknowledged that women would lead, not hot-blooded men. And since pure falcons were the most hot-blooded of all, it wasn't smart to let them reproduce with nobles of power. The fear ran deep that the actions of the past would be repeated. Besides, none could argue that the women did not do a superior job in making deci-sions and managing politics. Half of politics was dinner parties and hosting dignitaries anyway. Kings made for excellent bodyguards to their women, not to mention they raised the children, training them to defend themselves. Since Falconian men had naturally more physical energy, it only made sense that they would tend to the children.

The hall was filled, so packed with people that they spilled over into the courtyard outside. Rurik felt someone grab his arm. It was a light pull, and he automatically smiled, expecting to see a female beside him. He wasn't disappointed.

"Let me be your guest tonight, Commander," the petite blonde said, pursing her lips. She was dressed like the middle class, in a long tunic gown of light green. The sleeves tightly fitted to her wrists with decorative buttons up the side, and the rounded neck of the gown revealed a pleasing amount of cleavage. The bodice hugged her curves before flaring into a skirt at the lower hip.

"No, I want to be your guest, Commander," another woman said, a pout in her tone. He looked at his other arm, seeing a dark-haired temptress dressed very much like the lighter one, only in blue. First commanders, nobles and guests of honor would be seated in the hall, with others only as room permitted.

He wasn't surprised they knew his position, for

the two long, dark wings were hard to miss. Unlike the non-military Falconians, the warriors had wings. Pure born had them since birth, others grew them in time with the help of magic when they took their vow into the army. But, unlike the others, natural wings were darker and longer, reaching nearly to the ground when laid flat against the back.

The blonde put her hand on his chest, twining her fingers in the laces that held his tunic shirt together, which was more like a long jacket. The laces crossed down the front, from neck to waist, only to hang open at his legs so as not to hinder movement. The delicate silver and blue material was of the finest quality. As the woman's fingers traced the laces down to his waist, his body stirred in response, pressing against the tight black breeches he wore underneath.

"I'd do almost anything to see Princess Ari's Mating Day," the blonde said, batting her lashes with obvious meaning.

Rurik suppressed a frown as he thought of Ari. She'd been a stuck up child, and rumor had it she'd turned into an even more pretentious adult. Over the years, her true nature had been more than apparent. She'd signed the order to send his men on some of the worst missions. It was as if she wanted him dead and all because he had a little crush on her when they were children. Sure, he'd teased her, but mostly because he wanted her to loosen up.

Well, they weren't children anymore, and he'd outgrown Princess Ari. Now he was an acclaimed warrior of the Fifth, and if his keen sense of smell was any indication, these two women were definitely interested in helping him pass his time at the palace.

Lifting his arms, he hugged both women to his sides. "Now, ladies, don't fight. You can both be my guest. There is plenty of room on my lap for the two of you."

The women giggled. Rurik lifted his gaze briefly to the high throne in the middle of the hall, to where Princess Ari would drink from the Chalice. Let the princess have her mate, and blessed wings save the man chosen to it.

Already the hall was filled. Soon it would be time for the ceremony. Drinks were set out in goblets along the lower tables. Seeing some of his men in the back, he could tell they were already far into their cups by the way they moved and laughed. Rurik led the women alongside him toward the table.

"May the poor sod be whisked away on blessed wings, far from this palace and the arms of the princess," Lleu said, his second-in-command. The others laughed at the toast.

"Likely she'll dagger him in her bed tonight," Ivor added. The warrior was missing an eye, thanks to Ari's command to go into battle against Doc Truman and the Medical Mafia, who had tried to set up posts in their marshes. It wasn't that any of them were afraid of fighting the mafia, but at the time they'd been exhausted from defending the skies against pirates. It wasn't bad, except Terrick, Commander of the Fourth, later told them his men had been without a thing to do for months. Ari seemed to have it in for the Fifth.

"Only if it is a man from the Fifth," Rurik said, holding the two women to his side. "She does like to see our blood run, doesn't she?"

"Oh, have you been hurt in battle, Commander?" the blonde asked.

"See now, my most pretty feather, the commander merely floats in the sky as we warriors do all the work," Ivor said. He pointed meaningfully at the blue eye patch that covered the empty socket. "If it's stories of battle you'd like, then come sit by me. I've got many wounds that could use a female's gentle touch."

The women giggled.

"Get your own." Rurik laughed, taking a seat. With a swoop of his arms, he hauled both women onto his knees. "These two are my guests."

"Then you'd better take a drink, doves." Lleu slid a couple goblets in front of them, "Because I'm told the commander only looks cute after a few dozen goblets."

Rurik laughed at the good-natured ribbing as Lleu handed him a goblet as well, taking it off a nearby table.

"Hey, that's mine!" a burly warrior with long blond hair yelled.

"Go squawk to someone who cares," Lleu answered, just as surly.

Rurik closed his eyes, ignoring the men as the blonde kissed his ear. The darker woman reached down so that her hand rested against his inner thigh, her fingers tapping lightly as she took a long drink of the stout liquor. His arousal lifted in response, and he adjusted in his seat. Looking up at the empty throne, he thought that the ceremony couldn't come fast enough. He wasn't looking forward to seeing Ari again and the faster he could get out of her hall the better. And the sooner she was mated, the sooner he could forget all about her by burying himself in the two willing beauties before him.

Ari held her head high as she walked under the archway into the hall. She had waited in the hallway leading from her bedchambers until her father could escort her.

The red stone of the palace was adorned with the long purple flowering vines found in the prairies outside the battlements. They were strung into garlands along the tall ceilings and archways. Regal music sounded, announcing her arrival, as she walked down an aisle formed between the tables. Noble families and esteemed warriors filled the many tables around the center platform. All of them were well dressed, though some were more wealthily adorned than the others. At her appearance, those gathered in the packed hall stood in respect, though they didn't stop talking amongst themselves. It was an old tradition, one carried on for millenniums, supposedly long before her people had come to inhabit Falconia.

In the crowd, she was able to pick out a few of the better-suited males to be her husband. Sure, she had no real final say in the match, but usually the wishes of the bride were magically taken into consideration. The peasants rarely had trouble in mating to the men they loved. However, being as she was royalty, her future would not be so certain. If she had her choice, she would pick Lord Cyril of Karvof's son, Lynus. He was a little young, but very sexy and his father was a great nobleman with a lot of land close to the palace. Lynus smiled at her as she passed and she let the corner of her mouth lift in response. It wasn't love, but a prudent choice.

Suddenly, a round of feminine laughter caught her attention. It was just a little louder than the rest of the voices. She looked forward, but couldn't see who was making the noise. The music continued. When she looked at her father, so finely dressed in his dark-green robes, her smile widened. He led her to the steps that wound around the edge of the platform. Circling around it, they climbed to the top. From the vantage point, she was better able to see the crowd. Those standing tried to find seats as she waited before them. Slowly, she drew her gaze to the side, where the feminine laughter was coming from.

"Rurik," she whispered in surprise. She'd have recognized him anywhere. His chin-length dark brown hair was longer in the back, shorter in the front. The bangs framed his piercing black eyes. Ari had forgotten how much his eyes had disturbed her when they were younger.

"Ari?" her father asked. "Did you speak?"

"Nae," she answered, shaking her head. She forced her eyes away from Rurik, only to find them drawn back to him. Seven seasons had passed, nearly twelve years. How much time had changed things, and how little it did as well. It took all of Ari's willpower to continue to smile at the gathered crowd. He was much bigger than she remembered, with a harder edge to his features. However, that was not all that had changed.

Her jaw tightened in irritation. Rurik had two women on his lap, and they were indecently rubbing themselves against him. A pang of irritation shot through her at the sight. Not that she wanted Rurik or anything, she assured herself. It was just rude of him to act in such a way in her hall, on this day. Ari refused to notice a few of the other men who also sat with amorous women—some of whom were her honored attendants.

Rurik's eyes met hers and he stopped moving his hand on the dark-haired woman's back. Ari recognized the woman. She was the daughter of the palace baker and had already given herself to many of the men in the palace, including Ari's father in recent years if rumors held true. She looked at the king, wondering if he was jealous. He didn't even notice the woman.

Seeing movement at her side, she detected the Chalice attendant coming up the stairs. The music stopped, and the hall quieted. The young girl wore a white robe with a dark green and yellow stripe down the front. Her red hair hung loosely about her shoulders, nearly touching the floor.

Without a word, she held up the Chalice. Ari's fingers shook as she reached out. Hesitant, she took it. Feelings of hope and fear warred inside her. She'd managed to stay calm until this moment, but now her body shook from head to toe. She didn't want to drink and in a moment of panic she almost threw the Chalice to the ground in refusal. She looked at Lynus, wondering if she'd wake up next to him. Then, as she brought the cup to her lips and tasted the first sip of the magical pink liquid, her gaze darted to the side. Rurik's eyes were on her, steadily staring at her like everyone else's.

The liquid was unlike any she'd ever tasted, somewhat like punch and liquor and tingling herbs all in one. It slid thickly down her throat, and she coughed lightly, forcing herself to drink the entire concoction. A buzzing started in her ears as she drew the Chalice down from her mouth. She'd heard the sensations described, but feeling them was something else altogether. Her hands went numb, and she looked down in time to see them become transparent. The Chalice dropped, and the young girl leaned over to catch it. Suddenly, a bright white light bombarded her, and she heard droplets of rain seconds before the world went black.

4

Rurik bit the inside of his lip. His gut clenched as he watched Ari lift the Chalice to drink. Even from across the hall he could see that her eyes hadn't changed in their blue intensity. She saw him, he had no doubt, but she didn't smile, didn't show that she recognized him.

Part of him wanted to watch her, the beauty of her face, the soft curves of her body as she moved beneath the clinging material. The years had been kind to her, maybe too kind for they'd made her a gorgeous woman. He'd heard people speak of her beauty, but in his mind she was always the young girl, awkward and without power. He'd been attracted to her then, but now? Now she was a woman and attraction didn't even begin to cover what he felt.

The two women kissed his neck, but he didn't feel them, not really. Their hands were on his thighs, but in his mind he only wanted one person, and neither of them was she. His hands trembled, and he longed to wipe the makeup from her face, longed to run his fingers through her loosened hair.

Ari drew the Chalice from her mouth, her eyes wide as she looked down. The Chalice dropped from her hand, and he felt a strange tingling in his stomach, an almost nauseous sensation. Jealousy? Regret? Anger? A shiver worked over his spine, and he couldn't move.

"You're cold as ice." The blonde pulled away from him. "Commander, what is it?"

"He's freezing," the dark haired temptress added.

"Commander?" Ivor and Lleu said simultaneously.

Rurik opened his mouth to say he was fine, but a rush of air hit him, filling his lungs and knocking the breath from him, followed by a blinding light. He couldn't see a thing as the noises of the hall disappeared into the pounding sound of warriors' feet running over a battlefield seconds before they took to flight.

Then, suddenly, darkness replaced the light, a heavy, disorienting contrast. Soft cushioning pressed into his hands and knees and he realized he was bent over on a yielding mattress. Something warm was by his leg, and he reached over blindly to feel what it was.

"It's done," a woman whispered. There was relief in her tone. "I can't believe it's finally done."

His fingers ran over a leg, buried within a gown. It didn't take long to ascertain it belonged to the woman.

Nae, not just a woman. It belonged to...

"Ari?" he whispered.

Rurik drew his hand away as if burnt. Jerking back, he spread his wings slightly. They bumped an invisible boundary. He reached for it, feeling the air like a thick wall encircling them and keeping him trapped with the princess.

"Yea," Ari said. Her tone had deepened into an almost sultry, vixen's tone.

"Princess Ari?" he said, more to himself than to her.

"Yea, are you well, Lord?" she asked. "Did the

transition take you by surprise? What is your name? Who has the Chalice chosen for me?"

"I can't believe this. It's a mistake."

"The only way it's a mistake, Lord, is if you are..." the woman paused, "a pure blood."

Rurik froze and started to lower his naturally deep tone an octave more, but then stopped himself. He didn't expect Ari to remember his voice. "No taste for pure bloods?"

"What? Um, nae, it's just they can't rule."

His gut tightened. The way she said it, so knowingly, so finally, as if it were fact. His kind had ruled without problem until the end.

Rurik didn't know what came over him, but he was suddenly aroused with passion like he'd never known before. It was a mixture of desire, anger, the need to conquer once and for all. He didn't stop to think as he reached for her leg. Ari tensed beneath his hand, moaning softly. He could sense the need in her, the swift rush of passion at his touch. She was not immune to him.

When they were younger, he'd wanted to touch her so badly. He'd dreamed of her, masturbated to her, was tortured when she thought his love note to her was from another. How could he not lie about it though, when she'd laughed in his face at the thought of it being from him?

All the feelings he'd suppressed as a young man came surging forth, and he had to touch her, had to show her he wasn't the same person. Rurik had to show himself. He would make her respond to his touch, make her moan, make her fall in love before she ever saw his face and then...

He couldn't think beyond that part in his plan. The bed was soft, the area dark. Concentrating, he tried to see, using his naturally superior vision to pierce the darkness. It didn't work. He couldn't see through the magical barrier the Chalice created.

Running his hand down to her ankle, he pushed up the thin material of her gown. Even now he could picture her, standing by the throne, in the seductive, clinging gown, her long hair an impossible mess of twists to form a crown. He would've much rather seen the long red length down about her shoulders.

She was naked beneath the gown, and he lightly caressed his way up her leg, her thigh, her hip. The texture of her skin was like a dream. This couldn't be happening. Ari's breathing audibly deepened and the sweet smell she emitted made his insides tense.

"Hold." She sounded insecure. "A moment. Hold."

"You're beautiful, Ari." Rurik didn't stop. He couldn't. "When will we ever get another chance for this day? Let it happen. Let your mind think what it will."

Lightly, he kissed her hip, trailing his lips along her flesh. There was a bittersweet pleasure when she gasped. Would she be so willing, so passionate if she knew it was his lips that kissed her? Rurik hesitated, warring with himself. This was destined. The Chalice's magic brought him to her, gave her to him. But what if magic had gotten it wrong this time? What if the potion had been tainted?

Then this would be his only chance to have Ari. Years had passed, and he'd thought he was over her, but obviously that wasn't the case. Being a warrior, he knew how to take what he wanted. Rurik would not, could not back down.

Leaning back, he ripped her gown open along the front. The metal band around her body would be too hard to take off as it was bent to the shape of her chest and back. Tossing the material to the side, he closed his eyes, picturing her naked body before him.

Ari made small noises similar to prey cornered

by the hunter. Her legs were restless. As he leaned over, she reached to touch his chest. He stiffened, worried she might explore him and find the wings along his back. They'd give his position away, and she'd know he was a warrior and that a mistake had been made.

Stretching his wings back, he was careful not to lean too far forward as he kept his shoulders out of reach. Lifting her leg, he brought her ankle to his lips, kissing a hot, wet trail along her calf. Ari pulled on his shirt, tugging at the laces over his chest. When she couldn't work them free, but instead merely loosened them, she reached lower to his breeches.

Rurik dropped her leg, angling his body between her thighs. Pulling her down so her legs were bent over his, he caressed her hips and stomach, rubbing in slow circles up toward her glorious breasts. They were soft, pliable mounds in his palms, so big they overflowed in his hands. The gown she wore had hidden their true size from him, and he relished the discovery of her large nipples. The erect peaks begged for his lips, but he held back, fearful she might discover his wings if he leaned forward.

Her fingers skimmed over his clothed arousal,

the touch so hesitant yet unyielding that his cock couldn't help but fill to the point of explosion. By law, he knew she had only three lovers at most to minimize the risk of jealousy over her position, so it was possible she was nervous.

When she didn't free his erection, he reached for his own waistband and unfastened it. He pushed his breeches down just far enough to free his arousal for action. Her fingers glanced over the turgid flesh, and he nearly came.

Rurik grabbed her wrists, holding her arms to her sides as he finally leaned down. Worshiping her with his tongue and mouth, he licked and kissed her stomach and breasts, moaning softly just to taste her. Ari wiggled beneath him, her body so warm and eager. Not letting go of her arms as he dragged his tongue down to the apex of her thighs, he moaned louder as he tasted the sweet cream of her sex.

"Ah," she gasped. Rurik closed his mouth around her, licking and nibbling along her folds, only to suck her clit. "Oh!"

When the sound of her voice turned into incoherent pleas, and her body was thrusting in rhythm to his tongue, he knew it was time. Crawling on top of her, he slid her arms up, keeping her hands from exploring.

Leaning over, he pressed his mouth to hers. She jolted in surprise, and he used the chance to kiss her deeply. Her hands slipped from under his hold, reaching up to capture his neck. She kept him to her mouth as he spread her legs wider in invitation. In all his wildest dreams, he never imagined that Ari would be in his bed.

He hesitated, feeling a wave of guilt. The uncertainty was as unfamiliar to him as losing and he didn't know what to do. Rurik started to pull back. With a few words, he could drive her away forever. She wasn't his. He knew that. They came from different worlds, were born into different worlds. She was born to rule. He was born to fight.

"Nae," she whispered. "Stay."

Ari ran her hand down to his cock, rubbing it as she drew the tip forward to her sex. She offered her body to him, so sweet, so soft. He was powerless against her. She seized a part of him, a part that she'd always held, a part that kept him from all others throughout the many years. Rurik hadn't wanted to admit it his whole life. Once, he'd dared to hope, but he now knew how foolish hope was.

Once, he thought, taking what she offered. He

thrust forward, sliding in her cream as he pried her body open to his. The tight feel of her squeezed him, and he groaned in pleasure. His wings beat slowly, as he thrust, their subtle yet strong movement propelling him steadily in and out.

He couldn't take it. She jerked, tensing as she came. Grunting, he joined her in the blissful surrender of release, letting his seed spill within her, claiming her as his, marking her. Without thought, he collapsed forward, sure he'd never felt so scared or so happy in all his life. He tried to cling to the moment, knowing that it couldn't last, no matter how badly he wanted it to.

5

Ari couldn't believe how blessed she was. Her body sung with the intensity with which she came. The pleasure she'd given herself in the silent hours were nothing compared to the feel of live, confident flesh. The Chalice had indeed chosen wisely for her. Her mate was strong and fit. By his girth, she knew that it wasn't Lynus, or Ger, or any number of the men she'd considered over the last year. Nae, this nobleman was most likely a stranger to her. His voice held a trace of the familiar, but she couldn't place it.

She stretched her arms, feeling her loose hair about her shoulders. The crown had disappeared when she was brought to the bed. All that hard work for just a few moments in the hall. Such was the life of a ruler. She could spend hours getting ready for a ceremony that only lasted a few minutes.

Her heart pounded with the knowledge of what she'd done. She'd had sex with a man and didn't even know his name. Nae, not just a man, her mate. It was right that she was with him. The Chalice would not choose wrong for her. She had faith in that.

Ari didn't like how he held her hands down during sex, but perhaps he was nervous. Perhaps he had a scar he didn't want her to feel, or maybe he wasn't the best looking of men. It didn't matter. With a body that moved like his did, she could well get past an ugly face. Things like faces didn't matter to her. All she cared about was that he was kind and faithful and of a good, noble family.

Lightly, she ran her hands over his shoulders, curious to know more about him. He was breathing hard, and she smiled in giddy pleasure. "Mm, the Chalice chose..." Just then, her hand struck a protrusion along his back.

What...? A wing?

Jerking back, she pushed at his chest to get him off her. "What are you? A soldier?"

Suddenly, light flickered. Ari screamed in

protest, knowing that light would reveal them to the world as a married couple. She blinked as her eyes adjusted. Dark eyes met hers.

Nae, it can't be...

"Rurik?" she squeaked.

"Princess." Rurik tilted his head. His clothing was still on, only slightly disheveled. Though he looked directly at her, she couldn't read his closed expression.

Ari sprang into action, backing away from him. This was one man she didn't want to be in closed quarters with, let alone in the mating bed—*her* mating bed! She would've fallen, but the magical boundary held her up. Her back pressed against air.

"It's been awhile," he said.

"How...? What do you want with me? Why did you do this?" She couldn't get far enough away from him.

His eyes traveled down her body, and he looked amused. How could he look amused? Ari wanted to cry. He was mocking her. She could see it in the familiar smirk on his face. His body might have changed, but that look was the same. It mocked her. He'd always mocked her.

"I didn't do anything," he assured her, looking

very pleased with himself, "that you didn't beg to have done to you."

"I hate you," she whispered, for lack of anything better to say. "You haven't changed at all, have you? You're just a mean—"

"And yet you lay naked before me, like an offering ready to be fucked again."

Ari glanced down in horror, scrambling to pull the ripped pieces of her gown together to hide her body. The metal bodice helped hold them into place. "You haven't changed, have you?"

"Neither have you."

"Commander Rurik, leader of the great Fifth." She shook her head, still pressed against the invisible barrier. He kneeled before her, just as handsome as she remembered him being. "How dare you—*ah!*"

The barrier gave way, and she fell backward off the bed. Screaming, she flailed briefly in the air. Rurik's hand wrapped around her wrist, catching her. She bumped along the bed's hard side.

Suddenly, a stunted pounding started from below. Horrified, Ari looked down. Beneath her, a crowd stood tapping their feet in applause. Thankfully, she was turned toward the bed, and her torn gown was hidden from view.

"That was fast," she heard someone comment from behind. "The mating went well. I've never seen a couple come out so quickly."

"Pull me up," Ari whispered.

"What?" Rurik asked, smiling down at her.

"We'll bring a ladder, princess," someone offered. "No need to come down that way."

"Pull me up," she ordered, glaring at Rurik. "Now."

"Ask nicely," he grinned, holding her as if he could let her hang there all day without straining himself.

"Please," she said through gritted teeth. Something about this situation reminded her all too well of her childhood. Would the man never cease to embarrass her publicly?

Slowly, he pulled her up onto the bed, barely breaking a sweat. When she was safe, she jerked her arm away from him. It was a little too soon, and she nearly tumbled over the side again. This time, she caught herself, swatting at his hand as he tried to grab her.

"You haven't changed. Even as a child you had to torment me," she said. "This is just like that time you knocked wet cement on my head."

"We were using the buckets in training. You

shouldn't have been on the field," he protested, just like when they were younger.

"You didn't have to aim it at me," she ground out. Then, holding up her hands, she said, "There's no point in this. It's a mistake. We both know it's a mistake. We can't be mated. You're a soldier and soldiers can't rule. My true mate will be king."

"So soon you forget?" His grin was sinfully wicked, and she shivered at his meaning. The last thing she needed was a reminder of her wanton behavior. "The Chalice chose me."

"Come down, Ari," her father called. "Join the celebration."

Ari looked over, seeing the ladder. She reached across the bed to find one of the sleeveless robes that would have been left there for them.

"I can fly us," he offered. "It'll be faster."

"Nae," she said, too quickly as she tugged on the robe to hide her torn dress. The idea of his hands touching her made her skin tingle. She needed time to sort this out. "I'll climb."

His intense eyes bore into hers for a moment, and she had to look away first. He didn't say another word. Rurik's arms didn't move as his wings stretched to the side. They flapped, lifting his body up. He'd fixed his breeches when she wasn't looking and before she could speak, he was over the side, gliding to the floor.

"Oh," she sighed, shaking horribly. She was all too aware of the water wall arching overhead. They might not have heard her below, but they could see. She took a deep breath and then another. It would seem time had not changed much. Rurik could still thoroughly disarm her.

"Ari?" her father called. "Do you need assistance?"

"Nae," she yelled back. Tugging at the annoying coils fitted to her arms, she took them off. "I'm coming."

6

"Ari, I know it's strange to be mated to the commander, but the Chalice's magic has ultimate authority over our laws," the king said. Ari couldn't look at her father's eyes as she sat on a low, armless couch. They were in her father's chambers, near the library. Her father's belongings were being moved to a private room on the other end of the royal courtyard. By nightfall, this section of the palace would belong to her, as the new queen.

How could he agree to this? To Rurik? Ari shook her head in denial. "But he's a warrior, a pure shifter."

"Yea," the king agreed, nodding. "And pure bloods did rule the land at one time."

"And look what that brought us," she argued.

"We almost lost the planet to a bunch of over-grown, warmongering slugs."

"Gryger looked at the laws. There were none made saying pure bloods couldn't rule. It was just agreed that they shouldn't for a time and left at that. No one ever thought to look, because for the last several centuries the question never came up. However, he did come across a prophecy stating that one day, after the sins of the past could be forgotten, a pure blood would take the throne, combining the planet's strengths. Perhaps the time has come for them to reclaim part of the throne. Commander Rurik will make you a fine mate, and you will still have ultimate power over the planet."

"We both know Falconian prophecy is just a way for old men to ramble about what could happen and look smart." Ari shook her head. "Four thousand years ago they said a fiery ship would fall from the sky and alien men would steal away the daughters of noblemen."

"It could happen," the king protested.

"And yet it hasn't and we still have the law banning noblewomen from walking alone at night because of such nonsense."

"Ari," her father sighed heavily. "You must resign yourself to your fate. You chose to walk the path of the Chalice. You did not have to drink. If you would have poured the liquid on the floor, you would've remained unmated for the rest of your days. You knew the risk, and you accepted it."

"Right," she drawled. "I'm sure everyone would have loved that. There goes our family line, right onto the floor with the magic."

"It was your choice, whatever reasons you used to make it."

Ari frowned.

"Now, why don't you get dressed." Her father motioned toward the long tunic she wore. It was plain and white and not at all fitting for a princess about to become queen. "The hall is probably far into their cups, and I'd like to pass this crown to you so that I may join them."

7

Ari paced her chambers, doing her best not to look at the high bed. It did no good, for she couldn't stop her gaze from following the water wall up toward the ceiling, to where the site of her most unmentionable shame was reflected back to her.

Holy Comet, she'd wanted him. She still wanted him.

"Ari?" Vara spoke softly, her purple gaze shining with concern. Her friend held her coronation gown. It was much more concealing than the mating dress with the metal band.

"I was thinking about him, that's why the Chalice chose him," Ari said. "I'm being punished because I wanted revenge."

"It doesn't work like that and you know it." Vara laid the dark-red dress down on a low couch and joined Ari by the water wall. "The Chalice doesn't make mistakes."

"It did this time," Ari exclaimed.

"I'll admit it's strange." Vara sighed. "You should've seen the crowd when you two disappeared. First you, then suddenly those two women who were on..." Vara's eyes rounded in horror, and she covered her mouth.

"On Rurik's lap," Ari finished dryly.

"It just means he's virile," Vara offered.

"Great." Ari shook her head. "Not only am I mated to a commander who mocks me, he'll be sleeping with everything that comes within wingspan of him."

"Rurik isn't like that. He's not one of those. If anything, he does have honor. There isn't so much a blemish on his reputation."

"But why him?" Ari whispered. Taking her friend's hands, she held them tight.

"What aren't you telling me?"

"When we were younger and I thought Mikael gave me that love note."

"Yes?"

Ari took a deep breath. "You remember I told you how Rurik delivered it, or saw it, or I can't remember exactly how it happened that he was there when I discovered it because I was in such shock, but at first I thought it was from him. You know how I laugh when I'm nervous? Well, I laughed because I thought it was from him. I wanted it to be. But, he was just so mean about it, and that's when he told me it was from Mikael and I..."

"You never forgave him," Vara finished.

"He was always so mean to me," Ari said, her shoulders slumping by small degrees.

"And you hated him for it because you liked him."

Ari didn't want to delve into her buried emotions. She should've never started this conversation.

"That would explain why you've pined for him over the years. And why the Fifth gets all the dangerous missions."

"Nae, I don't—" Ari began, ready to deny that she sent Rurik and his men out on all the dangerous assignments. "Oh, blessed stars, I do, don't I?"

Vara nodded. "Half the noble court believes you want to have him killed."

"And the other half?" she asked, cringing.

"Think you want to have him maimed." Vara laughed softly. "That's why all the young boys pretend to be in the Fifth."

Ari rolled her eyes heavenward and gave a small laugh.

"So, now that we're talking about it, why do you send his men on the most dangerous missions?" Vara touched her shoulder, forcing Ari to look at her.

"The night before he flew out," Ari closed her eyes, remembering, "I heard him say he wanted nothing more than to have a long career filled with dangerous missions."

"I see." Vara grinned knowingly.

"What?" Ari lifted her hand. "Nae, never mind, I don't want to hear it. So, tell me, what happened in the hall. The two women did what?"

"Oh, yea, they screamed as they were both dropped on their asses. The crowd exploded into a frenzy when they discovered one of the soldiers had been chosen. Really, what could they do about it? Though, Lord Cyril did demand a reading of the laws and strangely Gryger was able to produce the book with little effort."

"What do you mean, strange?"

"He turned right to a prophecy that said—"

"Let me guess," Ari interrupted. "One day, after the sins of the past could be forgotten, a pure blood would once again take the throne, combining the planet's strengths."

"Yea, that is it." Vara nodded. "And that this day was the day that the prophecy said it would happen. When Lord Cyril heard that, he couldn't deny the validity of the marriage. In his irritation, he grabbed Lynus and together they left the palace."

Ari giggled. Then, as what her friend said sunk in, she scowled. "What did you say? My father and Gryger knew that today this would happen?"

"Appeared that way to me."

Ari crossed over to her gown and sat on it. "How could they not have warned me that I was to mate with Rurik? Do you think they told him?"

"I doubt it. The prophecy didn't say who would be picked, only that a pure blood would become king. And your father didn't tell you because he's not allowed to influence the mating decision. It is something you need to come to on your own, for your own reasons."

"You want to know my reason, Vara?" Ari gave a self-depreciating laugh. "I wanted sex."

Vara chuckled. "That's a good enough reason for me."

"Not just sex, but companionship. I told my father it was because I was duty bound to carry on the family name by having children, but the truth is I want to be held at night. I'm tired of being alone. I want a husband I can fall asleep with at night and wake up next to in the morning."

"And Rurik can't be that person? Ari, have you looked at him? He's gorgeous, he's built like a walking god, and he can fly. Can you imagine being in the arms of a soldier?" Vara giggled, kneeling by Ari's legs so as not to sit on the coronation gown. Taking Ari's hands, she said, "What more could you ask for in your bed?"

"He's not the holding kind," Ari said. "People who... Men like him... He's a soldier."

"Haven't you ever wondered what it would be like to have sex with a man who could fly? Hovering above the ground as they take you?"

"You should take a lover," Ari said.

"I haven't met any men who appreciate me, and I won't settle." Vara shrugged.

"I should have poured the Chalice out on the floor," Ari moaned, wanting nothing more than to hide.

"You should get dressed and face Rurik like an adult. You have grown up, chances are, he has too."

8

ARI STARED WIDE-EYED, stunned to silence as Rurik's bold fingers pressed between her thighs. Even through the thick red material of her coronation gown she could feel him rubbing along her slit, stirring her passions as she fought to keep them at bay. The dress was a beautiful tunic gown with a dark-red overskirt above a light cream underskirt. It fitted tight to her waist, held together by thick-corded ribbons that crossed under her breasts, supporting them. Her breasts were covered with a soft cream material that matched her underskirt. Suddenly, she wished she had a little more protection against the onslaught of Rurik's hands.

Oh, yea, she thought sarcastically as she

witnessed the childish taunting in his eyes, *he's really matured.*

"If you don't mind," she said under her breath, wiggling to be free. It didn't work. Her movements only caused his hand to rub all the harder. "I have a crown to accept."

"I'm surprised you didn't try and have the mating dissolved," he said, not letting her go. He had somehow snuck into her bedchambers. Her guess was he flew through a window in the shape of a falcon before making himself known. How long had he been there? Watching her dress? Hearing her conversation with Vara?

Nervously, she laughed. "I am a princess. I hold true to my word, Commander. I chose to drink from the Chalice and in doing so I have accepted the fate that is laid out for me."

"Huh, I thought it was because there was no defense. What, with the prophecy."

Her lips tightened in irritation.

Rurik laughed. His voice lowered, and his wings spread to the side as he leaned over to press his face close to hers. "Or was it because you liked it when I touched you?"

"I don't..." She couldn't finish the sentence. His

fingers felt too deliciously wicked against her pussy, and he was nibbling at her ear. "Mm."

"What was that, princess?" He kissed her neck. His wings came forward, their dark feathers looming to block out light.

"I..." she tried again, only to rock her hips against his hand. She felt safe next to his large body. All thoughts of duty and coronation left her as he continued his assault on her neck. He still wore the same clothes as before, and she ran her hands over the front of his tunic shirt, pulling at the laces.

"You felt me when I came inside you, didn't you?" His soft whisper was hot against her ear. "You feel my claim even now."

"Why are you doing this, Rurik? We both know you have no wish to be mated to me. Why aren't you trying to get out of it?" Ari bit her lip to keep from crying out. His fingers curled upward, making for an even deeper caress along her clit.

"Why else? For the power. Maybe now you will quit trying to have me and my men killed."

"What?" she gasped. He pulled back, his hand still intimately wicked along her sex, working her toward release through her clothing. His dark eyes pierced her with their intensity. "I nev-er, *oh.*"

"What was that, princess?" he demanded, keeping her trapped to his will.

"I said I never tried to have you killed." She couldn't think. Ari desperately wished he'd lift her skirts and take her as he had on the bed. His touch made it hard to concentrate, and yet she got the strange feeling that this was punishment as much as it was pleasure.

"I have scars on my body that beg to differ," he growled. "As do the bodies of my men."

Ari got a wicked flash of naked warriors in her mind, their hard, muscled bodies scarred. And in the forefront was Rurik, with his wings spread wide from his bare back.

"I didn't..." She tried to reason with him, but it was too hard to concentrate. Ari grabbed onto his shoulders, moaning softly as she rocked into his hand, completely accepting his touch.

"You did," he growled. "And I plan on making sure you grovel for my forgiveness by bathing and kissing each and every one of my scars. Then, you're going to kneel before me and ask me nicely to forgive you as you wrap your sweet lips around my shaft."

"I am to be queen. I don't kneel and I don't beg, not to anyone, not even a king."

"You'll do it, Ari, and you'll be thankful that I don't make you grovel in public. Too many times has death touched us, too many times by your will."

Her climax was close. "Nae. I won't...grovel."

Suddenly, Rurik pulled back, denying her his touch. She gasped as the pleasure stopped and she was suspended in the torturous moment before release. Her hands shook, and she thought of continuing on her own, but pride kept her hands away. Rurik was staring at her as she let her gaze roam over his body. His erection was hard, but he didn't act as if it affected him as he stood, arms crossed in displeasure.

"You'll grovel, princess, trust me on that point." He smiled, a deliciously wicked look as he licked his lips. "You'd better hurry. The hall is waiting to crown their new queen."

With that, he walked away, leaving her aroused and confused. What was that all about? Why did he stop? When she was alone, Ari suppressed a groan and reached between her thighs to replace where his hand had been. She rocked her hips, trying to end her own torment. Her body jerked, but it wasn't the same, it wasn't the intense orgasm promised with Rurik's touch, and it left her angry and disappointed.

WALKING AWAY WAS the hardest thing he'd ever done, but Rurik knew he had to leave her to think. He'd heard her talking with her cousin, Vara, about the past. To know she laughed at his note out of nervousness and not spite did something to him. But the note was only one thing in a trail of many childhood injuries they'd inflicted on each other.

His cock ached for release and he knew that if he'd wanted, he could've pressed his mate against the wall and taken his pleasure in her sweet, wet sex. Holy stars, her breasts looked good, pressed up by the tight corset of her bodice. This dress did nothing to hide the large, full shape of the mounds. It was all he could do not to turn around and rip the cream linen open so that they might spill out for his pleasure while still being held high by the tight bodice.

But he couldn't. The way he saw it, there was only one way to find happiness with the lot the Chalice had drawn for them. He had to show her that he was a commander. That he could respect her, just as he could be trusted to lead her. All their lives, she'd acted better than him, been told she was better than him. Over the years, it was her deci-sions that controlled his life. Well, it was time for the tables to turn. He would teach her to grovel so that she could walk beside him as an equal. Rurik would show her how much she wanted him, would make her admit to those desires. He'd long ago admitted to his.

9

THE CROWD TAPPED their feet in applause for the longest of time, happily receiving Rurik as their king and as her chosen mate. She'd expected more of an uprising, but it appeared the people were really ready to forget and forgive the unfortunate incidences that took the pure bloods from rule. Could it be the prophecy was right? Were they more than just ramblings of old men? She would make a point of studying what the prophecies said a little more closely after she took her official rule.

Falconian ceremonies were simple, and her father had only to take his crown and place it on her head for it to be over. There were no words, as the symbolic passing of the crown was enough to convey what was happening, just as her drinking from the goblet had been enough to seal her fate to Rurik.

Ari was all too aware of her new mate next to her, his taller height towering above her. She waited as Rurik was given a smaller crown. Suddenly, his wings spread wide, and the hall went crazy with excitement, pounding their feet and cheering for their new king.

Show off, she thought. Her body was still tense from her almost climaxing, and she resented Rurik for starting something he didn't finish. After the ceremony, music was played, and couples took to dancing as well as drinking. Ari was amazed to see her father amongst the other nobles, acting more carefree than she'd ever seen him. She didn't dance, but instead sat on her throne watching.

"Do you wish to join them?" Rurik asked from her side. His voice was deceptively soft, and she stiffened to hear the niceness of his tone.

Blinking, she looked at him. "Nae. It isn't done."

"According to...?"

She opened her mouth to speak, but the truth was, she didn't know. It really wasn't written in law that she couldn't dance or do any number of things, it was just traditionally how it was done.

"I propose, my queen…" Rurik began. The title still jarred her slightly, though she'd been prepared to accept it.

"Yes?" she breathed, unable to form a solid word.

"I propose that it's time to let a little more blood into the rule," he said.

"What do you mean?" Ari wrinkled her brow in confusion, studying him.

"When my kind was banished, it was thought that women, who had more control over their passionate blood, should rule for a time. They have, and your family has done a good job of it. Nevertheless, the throne lacks passion. Perhaps it's time to let some of the fun back into ruling Falconia. Our people were never meant to be passionless, Ari. Our ancestors ran from passion because of what it brought. Perhaps it's time to reclaim some of it."

"So you're saying…?" she asked, thoroughly intrigued by what he suggested.

"I'm saying, let us join our people and dance. There is no shame in a queen enjoying her life. Come, let us flush that perfect complexion of yours and make you break a sweat."

"I, ah, sweat," she protested, even as she allowed him to touch her hand. "I exercise."

"Dance with me," he insisted. "Let us start this reign with blood in its veins."

Ari was too stunned by the prospect to protest as he pulled her to her feet. The hall suddenly lost some of its buzz as he led her along the stairwell that wound down the platform to the floor. She was well aware of the eyes on her.

"Rurik," she pulled at her hand, trying to stop him, "a queen doesn't..."

"A queen *hasn't* in a long time," he corrected. "Do you really want to live your ancestors' lives? Or would you rather live the life of Queen Ari and her hot-blooded king?"

There was something intimate and accepting to the way he linked their names together, and she would've agreed to almost anything at the moment. He led her down to the hall. The musicians had stopped, looking unsure.

"Play something lively," Rurik yelled, as if commanding all those around him. "The new queen wishes to dance with her people."

Ari's stomach tensed, and she expected a riot of outrage. Instead, no one seemed to care that it wasn't done. They cheered, several reaching out to pat her on the back in welcome. Rurik grinned, pulling her close as a lively beat started over the hall. She felt the definition of his tight muscles against her body, pressing to her breasts, which suddenly felt heavy and achy against him.

Soon she was swept into a whirl of turns and spins. Rurik led her to skip along the floor in one direction, only to spin her around and lead her in the other with his chest to her back. She'd seen the dance performed several times but had never done it herself—well not any place where she could be seen—and never with a partner.

Rurik was a wonderful dancer, lifting and leading her around the floor so that it looked as if she'd been dancing for years. Ari laughed, feeling carefree, reveling in the hard pumping blood in her veins. Rurik was right. This was exactly the kind of thing her rule needed. Suddenly, the burden of being responsible for so much lifted and she felt as carefree as a peasant.

"It's crowded," Ari said after several songs had passed in lively dancing. He kept her close, going so far as to lift her feet off the floor to keep time with the music. "And hot."

Rurik danced her past a table and grabbed an unused goblet set up at the end. Slowly, he handed it to her. Ari swallowed the stout liquor, gulping it down. It wasn't the same kind she was served as royalty. There was a heady flavor to it. Rurik took the goblet when she finished and set it down, before grabbing another and offering it to her. Ari drank that one as well. She hadn't eaten too much, and the instant effects of the strong drink in her blood were easy to feel.

"Fifth," Rurik yelled. "Into dance formation."

Ari tensed in surprise at the barking order, her eyes round as she tried to pull away from Rurik. He held her tight, grinning widely.

"Hold on, my queen," he said, before leaping up into the air over the crowd. Ari gasped, clutching onto his shirt. As he spun her, she realized he'd merely moved her out of the crowd to give them more room to dance.

"But my skirt," she protested, wondering if people would see her naked body beneath if they looked up.

"We'll be spinning too fast," he assured her. Several of his men had gone up into the air at his yelled command, and she saw the stunned expression of the other women as they were flown around the room in the dance.

Below them the crowd cheered, blurring with

the sound of the music. Ari's head spun from the liquor, and she laid it on his shoulder as he twirled her around. Closing her eyes, she held on, feeling the subtle shift of his wings as they moved. It was arousing, yet frightful, to be under his complete control. Ari couldn't fly, and if he were to let go, she'd fall.

"I'm curious," Rurik said.

She didn't lift her head. Unbidden, the deliciously erotic movements of his body against hers began stirring her passions once more. Wicked thoughts entered her mind, so arousingly wicked that she didn't want to stop and think. Vara had mentioned the idea of having sex while in flight, and she could see how exotic and wonderful such an idea could be.

If they were alone, she would've forgotten who he was and would've demanded he have sex with her right where they were. Good thing the crowd was there to keep her at bay. His earlier words entered her head, words about wanting her to humble herself before him. Where did that man go? That impossible, controlling man? The Rurik who held her didn't remind her of him. Nae, this Rurik was almost sweet, gentle, fun. This wasn't the man who demanded she grovel or the boy who teased her mercilessly as a child.

Her breathing deepened. Would it be so bad to explore the scars on his body? He might think he was punishing her, but it would give her ample time to explore his bare form. She did want to see him naked. Her fingers kneaded against his shoulders, and she wished she could remove the shirt off his muscular chest. Every inch of him was solid and firm, just as a warrior commander should be. The breeze around them stirred with the wings of Rurik and his men, but the commander's wings moved with such light grace that she felt as if she were floating on air.

When he shifted, his body would become compact as his shape molded into the form of a true falcon. She'd seen the men shift in the past, for they often entered the palace and left it in such a way. It allowed them to fly faster and more efficiently over long distances. But she'd never seen a naked pure blood before. When they shifted, the fibers from their clothing were absorbed into the body so they'd have clothes when they un-shifted.

Ari held him tighter, very aware of how her breasts rubbed against him. Her nipples ached for his attention and moisture gathered within her thighs, readying her body for his claim. The feel-ings felt too wonderful to fight though she knew she should grasp onto whatever dignity she could.

"I'm curious," he repeated. Ari had no idea how much time had passed since he'd last spoke.

"Yea?" she answered.

"What are your powers, my queen?" he asked. "Word was spread that you got them, but none have seen what they are besides a select few."

Ari laughed but didn't answer him. "Don't you worry. They are great."

"Show me," he said.

"Nae," she answered, not wanting to take her mind off the feel of him pressed against her. She just wanted to enjoy the moment. "I just want to dance."

"Then tell me what they are," he said.

"I can control water." It was an oversimplifica-tion of all she could do, but she didn't want to get into all the little nuances of her gift. She could snake it through a room, or make it dance, or create a wall that never fell. She could call upon the ocean to give her its jewels if she wanted—though she never would because it would take jobs away from some of the sailors.

"Will you show me later?" he asked.

"Perhaps." She lifted her head. "If you beg me to."

"How soon you forget, but it is you who must beg me." As if to punctuate his meaning, he adjusted his hips, letting her feel the full length of his arousal. He was as aroused as she. Ari tried to wiggle away from the prominent erection, but being as they were in the air, there was no place for her to go but down. "Are you ready to retire, my feather?"

"Not with you," she quipped, trying to think straight, trying to remind herself that she disliked him.

Rurik frowned. His wings worked furiously as he turned them around in faster circles.

"Hold," she protested. "Please, you're making me dizzy."

Suddenly, he stopped spinning. Before she could catch her breath, he beat his wings hard against the air, sending them speeding over the hall toward the entrance to her princess chambers.

"You DIDN'T MIND my touch earlier."

Ari blinked, surprised at his abrupt words as he set her down on the mattress of the mating bed. She'd barely had time to part the water to let them through without getting wet, as they sped into the chambers. Looking down over the edge, she knew she couldn't easily get down without help. Her belongings had already been moved during the coronation, and the room seemed empty.

"Whose idiotic idea was the high bed anyway?" she mumbled.

"When the pure bloods ruled, they were not an issue," he said. "They were to protect the royal family against invaders."

"For a warrior, you're pretty smart," she said.

"You know, feather, that might be the first compliment I've ever gotten from you." He reached for her, touching her face in a gentle caress.

Ari's head was a little fuzzy from the drinking and dancing. Already her flesh stung with the pleasure of his touch. She wanted him. There was no denying it. The bed reminded her of how they'd come together, in the dark, his hands pinning her down. She wanted to explore him, to see him, to watch his face as he entered her body.

Unhurriedly, she reached for his waist and gently set to work on the laces. Tugging on them, she pulled them free, slowly revealing his stomach and chest. The backs of her hands glided over his taut flesh. Once she'd finished, she crawled to his back and set to work on the laces beneath his wings.

Rurik pulled the shirt over his head and tossed it aside, only to sit back on his knees. Ari stared at his dark, beautiful wings. They protruded out of his back, held to the side by strong muscles. Running her hands over the soft feathers, she shivered. Then, finding the tanned flesh of his back, she touched a long scar that ran down along his spine. She leaned forward to lick the scar as she dragged her mouth over him. Rurik tensed, his wings spreading wider as her mouth neared the back of his neck. Smaller scars puckered his skin, and she sprinkled hot, wet kisses over them.

She called the water from the wall, urging a tiny strand to form and heat so it would be warm. Like a liquid snake, it slithered through the air. Rurik gasped as she controlled it easily with her mind, making it glance over his chest to where she couldn't see. It didn't matter. If she wanted it to touch his nipples, it would, such was her power over it.

When she'd made her way kissing and licking his back and arms, she slowly moved to stand before him. The water had left small trails over his chest. She urged the water to form a hand. With it, she cupped his face and bid him to stand before her. He did and she instantly leaned in to kiss his chest, teasing the scar she found with her tongue. The water trail held still as she lightly sucked a hard, wet nipple between her puckered lips.

Rurik's hands found her arms and he began pulling at her gown to undress her. Her shoes were gone, but she didn't remember taking them off. She pulled back only long enough to lift the gown over her head and toss it aside. Her long hair tickled her back as she pressed her body against his. The heat of him instantly made her nipples into hard beacons. She moaned, wiggling her hips as his hands glided over her naked ass. He pulled her cheeks, spreading her from behind ever so slightly as he massaged in hard, perfect circles.

Trembling, she reached for his cock, stroking it several times through his tight breeches. It wasn't enough. She needed to feel the turgid flesh in her palms. Eagerly she tugged at his waistband. Rurik kicked off his boots, before helping her push his pants down from his hips. Soon he was standing gloriously naked before her, his arousal thick and long and ready.

Moaning, she kneeled, kissing each and every scar she saw, bathing them with her tongue. His sinewy flesh was salty-sweet and so very addictive. She ran her hands over his tight ass, squeezing and caressing every hot, hard inch of it before moving over his large thighs.

She drew the water snake forward, heating it before urging the liquid to wrap around his cock. It shaped over him like a cocoon, ringing around his shaft and balls. Rurik gasped, thrusting lightly in the air. It was a gorgeous display, seeing his beautiful body strained with passion. She made the water rush around him, fast and vibrating. Ari's breath deepened at the erotic show and she urged the water back against the sensitive flesh between his thighs, buried behind his balls. She'd used water for pleasuring herself many times, urging it between her thighs. Hot moisture gathered in her slick folds, both from her body and the water. The liquid did not enter her, but instead vibrated and rushed over her clit in waves.

Grabbing his hips, she let the water part over his cock to make way for her mouth. She concentrated the liquid on her body and his balls, as she licked the thick tip of him.

"Ah-ah," he gasped, as she sucked him between her lips.

Since he was wet from the water, he slid easily into her mouth. Her nipples ached for attention, and she made the water caress her there as well. The more aroused she became the harder and faster she sucked him, rolling her tongue over his thick shaft, trying to fit him deep.

She moaned, reaching to grab his wet balls in her hand through the vibrating water. Rurik's fingers buried themselves in her hair and he jerked his seed hard into her mouth. She drank him down, sucking on him for more.

With a groan, he pulled her off. The water

retracted back toward the wall, all except the stream along her clit. She closed her eyes, reaching for her own breasts.

"Let me," he said, breathlessly. Rurik had her on her back before she could stop the water from behind. It squished against the bed, wetting the sheets. She let go, only to discover how much better his mouth felt against her pussy. Warm hands cupped her chest, playing with her nipples. "I love your breasts."

Keeping one hand on her chest, he drew the other to her sex. His mouth did wonderful things to her clit as he audibly drank her cream. Suddenly, a thick finger thrust up into her, and she tensed in pleasure as Rurik took her with his hand and mouth. He knew just how to touch her and it wasn't long before she was coming, crying out his name and begging him not to stop what he was doing. When the tremors subsided, Rurik collapsed alongside her quivering body.

11

Ari wasn't sure when it happened, but somehow she'd fallen into a blissful sleep. When she awoke, it was to find Rurik beside her, his body aroused and pressed along her back. He was kissing her neck and ear.

"I want to be inside you," he whispered. "I want to feel the tight silk of your sex wrapped around me."

She opened her mouth to speak, but suddenly a shout from below stopped her.

"My queen, my king!"

Ari reached around for something to hide her body with, automatically forcing the water arch down so it didn't reflect her body to whoever was below.

"Ari?" the person called again and she realized it was Vara.

"Vara?" Ari asked, leaning over the side. She must've left the door open in Rurik's flight to get her into his bed.

"Ari, it's Lord Cyril. He says he found a way to end your mating to a pure blood. He's here with his son, trying to lay claim to the throne."

Rurik tensed behind her. Ari blinked, suddenly feeling sick to her stomach. She looked at her mate, her heart squeezing in her chest at the idea of losing him. But what would he choose? He was a warrior. Could he be happy in a queendom at her side? Or did he long for the open air and freedom of being a commander with his men? Would he choose her? Would he leave her if he had the choice?

"Rurik," she whispered, not knowing what else to say. Did she confess to him, let him know how she felt, that she wanted him, had always wanted him?

"Duty calls, my queen," he said, his words clipped. Then, louder, he yelled, "We'll be right down. Please wait outside."

"Yea, king," Vara answered respectfully.

Not knowing what to do, Ari looked around. Weakly, she said, "My dress."

He had his breeches already pulled on and was working on his boots. "I'll fly us down. Come here."

Ari wrapped her arms around his neck at his bidding, and he glided them toward the floor.

"One day and already someone challenges the throne," he said wryly as he set her down.

Ari wanted to say something to him, wanted to ask him if he could possibly be happy as her king, but the words wouldn't come. She opened her mouth, but she felt like a young, tongue-tied girl and all the insecurities that came with such an age rushed over her.

"Did you want to say something?" His eyes narrowed. He looked like the hunter. Would the hunter be happy out of the hunt, or would he resent her for keeping him?

She knew her answer. A man like Rurik wouldn't want to be caged, even if the bars were gilded. She'd felt the freedom of his arms, but knew that was only a dance, one moment out of a lifetime of serving her people. She looked at his wings, knowing they'd only remind them both of what he had to give up against his will.

"You're free," she whispered, leaning to pick up her undergown. She slipped it over her head, trembling.

"What are you saying?"

"You're free, Rurik. This is your chance to get out of this. No repercussions will come of it. In fact, Lord Viceious will be stepping down soon as Supreme General. The job will be yours if you want it. As Commander of the Fifth, you and your men have more than earned the honor. None will protest."

"You mean you'll be free," he said, a severe frown crossing his face.

"The life of a queen is hardly freeing." She pulled her gown over her head, before working her hair out of the back.

Walking to the water wall, she looked at her reflection. Her cheeks were flushed with sleep, and her hair was a mess. Running her fingers through the locks, she sighed. It was no use. She needed a brush, and her belongings were elsewhere in the palace. Regardless, she did the best she could with it before turning back to him.

"Your motives in this are hardly pure. You wish to buy me off with your offer of Supreme General, don't you?"

Ari swallowed nervously, avoiding his eyes. It wasn't a complete lie, though she wouldn't have used the phrase "buy him off". True, as Supreme General he would come to the palace and be her liaison to the troops. The offer was selfish of her. She wanted him close. Now that their bodies had joined, she knew she needed more of him. If it was decided that she remain unmarried or even in the unlikely occurrence that she took another husband, she knew in her heart that she'd take Rurik back into her bed—scandal or not.

"You haven't changed, have you? You're still the spoiled little princess who is too good for us soldiers." His wings stretched, his whole form tense with anger.

"What?" she gasped, ready to defend herself.

"Don't bother, my queen." The words were tight. "You've made your point." Then, stepping closer, he growled, "But just remember, this pure blood's hands were all over your body and you begged for me to touch you."

Ari blinked in confusion. Why would she ever want to deny it?

Rurik's body shifted. His eyes narrowed, and his nose and mouth molded into a beak. Feathers sprouted over his body, and his wings beat against the air. Soon he hovered in the air before her, his body compacted into a large bird of prey. With a fierce speed, he turned and flew out of the chambers toward the hall. She was still staring after him, long after he was gone.

12

RURIK WAS LIVID. Did their time together mean nothing? Was she so ready to throw him back at the first chance that presented itself? Oh, and offering him the position of Supreme General. That was a nice touch. It was the highest honor for a man like him. Or, it had been until he'd become king.

Coming to the hall, he instantly saw Lord Cyril and his simpering son, Lynus. It was no secret that Ari spent time with the young man. He hadn't wanted to listen to rumors, but her name was spoken and he couldn't help but hear whatever was said about her.

Swooping past the nobleman's head, he glided up toward the throne. He didn't bother to shift as he perched on the back of the high chair. It was early in the morning and he realized they'd slept all night in each other's arms. What was odd was he never lost track of time like that. Ari just did something to him. She always had.

If she would just want him as he wanted her. If she would but ask him, he'd lay down his life. But she didn't seem to want his heart or his life. Nae, but she'd wanted his sex badly enough. It was a bittersweet victory.

The former king was seated close to Lord Cyril. The royal librarian was with them, leaning over an old, weathered piece of parchment. Rurik turned his head, listening to them speak. Their tones were low, but he could make out their words easily enough.

"See, there, it says 'in a time that the deeds of the pure bloods can be forgiven,'" Cyril said. "Well, that's simple. I for one don't forgive them. And, if a noble house cannot forgive the deeds, then surely there are others who feel the same."

"It doesn't specifically say 'forgiven by the house of Cyril of Karvof,'" the old king argued. If he'd been able to, Rurik would've smiled. The old king had always shown him favor, even as a child. He'd taken him under his wing, so to speak, and taught him to be a man. "I think Commander Rurik to be a fine choice. Besides, the magic of the Chalice should not be challenged."

"Should not, not cannot," Cyril argued. "I say it's been tampered with. Something was wrong with the magic. The old wizard was sick. There has to be an explanation."

"And let me guess," the old king mused. "You propose we set aside this decision for what? To pave the way for your son Lynus?"

"Queen Ari had shown great favor for my son and Lynus would make a fine king." Cyril didn't miss a beat. "He's noble of birth and temperament. He's politically minded. He has already met with many of the dignitaries that come to the planet."

"And I say Rurik can meet those dignitaries and whatever graces you think him to be lacking can be learned." The old king shook his head.

"Forgive me, old highness," Cyril sneered, "but the decision and translation of these scrolls are no longer yours. They are the queen's. We'll see who she picks—some barbaric commander or my son, a true king."

Rurik squawked in anger at the slight. Diving down from his post, he swiped past Lord Cyril's head and grabbed a talon full of his hair. With a mighty pull, he yanked it out and flew out of reach.

The old king laughed. "I think someone doesn't like being called barbaric, Cyril."

Cyril growled in outrage, rubbing his head. "My point exactly. Barbaric!"

13

"WHAT IS THIS?" Ari appeared, her voice calmly coming over the barren hall. "What reason have you to interrupt my morning, and so early at that?"

Even disheveled, she kept her chin up, doing her best to look regal.

Seventy-five percent of being royalty was in the attitude. Walking slowly, as if she hadn't a care in the world, she made her way up to her throne. She'd found her crown on the floor along with Rurik's. They must have lost them the night before in his wild flight toward the bed, but she hadn't realized it until she found them in the hall.

As she came up the circular stairs, her eyes landed on the falcon perched on the back of the king's chair. She shivered, automatically knowing it was Rurik. She would've recognized those eyes anywhere, shifted or not.

"My queen," Cyril said, bowing. His son was behind him, and they were joined by her father and Gryger, the librarian.

"Lord Cyril," she said, nodding at him to speak. She stared down her nose at him. Inside, she shook violently. She didn't want to let Rurik out of their mating, but he'd left too fast and she hadn't had time to ask him what he wanted.

"May I be blunt?" Cyril asked.

Ari nodded. "Please, do."

"Though a great soldier, Commander Rurik is hardly a man fit to be king. He's a pure blood, and as we all know and accept, that comes with a certain amount of," Cyril paused, rubbing his head, "hot-blooded temperament."

"Yea," Ari agreed. Her stomach tensed. That's one of the things she liked about him—his hot-bloodedness. Her thighs tingled, and moisture gathered in her sex as she thought of just how wild he could be. Damn Lord Cyril for interrupting what had promised to be a very enjoyable morning. A little harshly, she demanded, "And?"

"It is my feeling that we don't have to accept the Chalice's decision. I have proof," he pulled a folded parchment from his jacket and held it up, "that the Chalice's magic has been overturned in the past and a marriage dissolved to the agreement of both parties."

"Give me that," Gryger demanded. The normally mild-mannered librarian unfolded the parchment and began reading to himself. "But, this is your great-great-grandfather's..."

"Yea, it is, but it proves that marriages can still be dissolved happily," Cyril interrupted.

"I know this case. The wife died within the year," Gryger said. "The dissolvement wasn't recognized by all."

"Completely unrelated. She was happy before she died." Cyril took the parchment back and stuck it into his pocket.

"The king—" Cyril began.

"Gentlemen, I do not have patience for this," Ari said. "Your point please, Lord Cyril."

Looking pleased with himself, he said, "I propose you dissolve your marriage to Commander Rurik by royal decree and choose for yourself a proper husband of noble birth."

Ari looked at her father. "Are you aware, Lord Cyril, that my father was a farmer and not of noble birth when the Chalice chose him for my mother?"

"What? I..." Cyril looked around, stunned.

"And you propose to insult my father?" she asked.

"Nae, nae," Cyril insisted. "I meant no disrespect to the old king."

"Lord Cyril," Ari stood.

"Yea?"

"Leave," Ari commanded.

"Excuse me?" The nobleman looked around the empty hall.

Ari felt a stirring by her side and paused to see Rurik standing beside her. His clothing looked impossibly perfect, and she assumed that was partly due to the shifting.

"I don't want you..." she started to speak, hesitating before looking up into Rurik's eyes. When he was in falcon form, it had been easier for her to ignore that he was there, right beside her as she tried to say what she needed to. But now, seeing him, she knew what she had to say was for her mate's ears, not Lord Cyril's. She didn't care about Cyril or his politics. She didn't want Lynus for a mate. She only wanted Rurik, and it was time she told him, flat out, what she felt. If he rejected her, then at least she would know she tried. He looked away. Her heart beat wildly. She had to say it. "I don't want you to leave, Rurik."

His hot gaze turned back to hers, his eyes narrow slits as he studied her. "What did you say?"

"I don't want you to leave me. Please, don't leave me to rule alone," she whispered, stepping closer to him. "I want...I want y..."

"Ari?" He started to lift his hand. It hovered by her cheek before falling away, not touching her.

"I want you to be king. I mean my king. I want you to be my king. I've tried, but I can't think of a single thing to entice you into wanting the job. It's not battles, and I know you wanted to be in battle, but... Stay anyway. Rule with me." Ari's whole body trembled, and she wasn't sure whether to laugh or cry. Why didn't he speak? She so wanted him to speak and yet at the same time she was terrified by what he might say. "Bring blood to the throne."

"You wish for blood?" He laughed softly, a small smile curling the side of his mouth for a brief second, so brief she wondered if it was just hopeful wishing on her part.

"Nae, yea, I mean your blood, pure blood. I mean," she took a deep breath, "love me."

He took a step closer, tilting his head to the side. "Did you just say...?"

She nodded. "Yea. Love me, Rurik."

"As my queen?" he asked, his expression guarded as if he was purposefully misunderstanding her.

"As my mate," she said, only to backtrack. "Unless... Yea, as a queen."

Finally, he touched her, and she felt her entire being freeze in wonder. Leaning forward, he shook his head. Her heart dropped. "Foolish little feather, don't you know? I've loved you since we were children."

Ari gasped. "You're just saying that. You could barely stand me as a child."

"Then why did I write that note for you?"

"You? That note was from you?" She gasped in surprise. "But, you said..."

"I remember what I said, but you laughed at it. What else could I do?" His fingers ran over her cheek. "Why do you wish for me to love you, Ari? You have people to love you as a queen. I need to hear you say it."

"Because I love you, Rurik. I always have. I'm sorry I laughed at your note. I was stupid, nervous, a young stupid nervous girl and I—"

His crushing lips cut her off as he seared her mouth with his, delving his tongue to conquer and explore her depths. Ari moaned, grabbing onto his arms for support as her knees buckled beneath her.

"Ah, Ari?"

She ignored the voice.

"Ari?"

Again, she ignored it. Rurik's kiss felt so right. Her body stirred to his.

"Daughter!" her father yelled, finally getting her attention. She blinked, turning to look at him in stunned surprise. "You want to finish..." He motioned to a red-faced Lord Cyril.

"I was finished," Ari glared down at the man.

"But..." Lord Cyril stared at her, his mouth working, but no sound coming out.

"I said get out," Ari ordered.

"You heard my queen," Rurik barked. Instantly the man rushed from the hall.

Ari laughed. "I should be upset that he didn't listen to me when I commanded it."

"Don't worry," Rurik said. "I'll teach you how to scare people."

"Mm." She wrinkled her nose before leaning forward for his kisses once more. Rurik loved her. The knowledge poured over her, giving her more pleasure than she ever dreamed possible. "No need. You can scare them for me."

He stepped forward, walking her with him toward the edge, but she wasn't scared. Looking deep into his eyes, she trusted him with more than her life. She trusted him with her heart.

"I love you," she said. "I've wanted to say that for a long time."

"I love you," he answered, leaning as if to kiss her.

She pulled back. "Fly us to our royal chambers this time, okay?"

He nodded, laughing softly as he turned directions and walked her the other way.

"Come on, Gryger," her father said. "Let's leave these two alone."

"Where would you like to go, highness?"

"Old highness," the old king corrected. "I'm thinking to the country. There has to be a woman or two out there that doesn't know I was king."

Ari giggled, not taking her eyes off Rurik. He leaped, hooking a leg around hers to hold her close as he carried her through the air toward their new room.

Rurik landed by a low canopied bed. She smiled, glad it was closer to the floor than the mating platform had been in her old chambers. Paintings of Falconian men hovering above their women as they took to the sky decorated the top panels of the room. The deep colors were brilliant in their rich tones. Dark wood from the black trees that grew in the nearby forest had been used to carve the canopy and matching panels along the wall. Some of the panels would lead to secret rooms within the palace, but she wasn't sure which ones. The wood was polished to a black gleam, reflecting the soft light that came from the high palace windows. An archway led to a similar dressing room.

The air smelled sweet and welcoming, having been scented by the palace servants. Soft material met her hands as he laid her down on the bed. The coverlet was new, as was the rest of the bedding.

"I'm sorry for all that was done between us," she said.

"As am I, but we were children." Rurik kissed the corner of her mouth and moaned softly. He ran his hand over her side to touch a breast through the material of her dress. "And you have grown into a fine woman, Ari."

She giggled in pleasure. "And you make a very fine figure of a king, Rurik."

He kissed her again, this time deep and long. His tongue edged along her lips, begging entrance into her mouth. She sighed, taking him in as his fingers explored her body. She wanted him, and it wasn't long before she was aroused and wiggling for more.

"What about those women on your lap? Are you sorry for them?" Ari asked, breathing deeply. She closed her eyes as he pulled at her skirt.

"What women?" he groaned, kissing her neck.

"At the mating... Oh, that feels really nice." She parted her thighs, allowing his fingers access to her slick folds. His thumb pressed into her clit, rubbing in small circles.

"There are no other women but you, Ari," he said.

Ari laughed. "That's the perfect answer."

"It's also very true."

Rurik continued to kiss her neck as he worked his hand against her sex. Ari grabbed onto his shoulders, pulling at his shirt but unable to get it off.

"Undress for me," she ordered, eager to see and feel him once more.

He quickly obeyed. She watched him, squirming restlessly on the bed. As he reached for his pants, she hurriedly pulled at her own gown. Naked, she tossed the dress aside and lay back down. He was glorious, with his dark hair and eyes, his impressive wings spread behind him. With a wickedly playful gleam in his eyes, he reached behind him and pulled out a feather. Angling it toward her, he grinned as he brought it to her leg. The light, tickling caress made her jolt as it worked its way up her inner thigh. He stroked it over her sex and circled her breasts in tantalizingly flawless sweeps across the nipples.

She touched his naked thigh, loving the feel of his flesh on her palm. He was hot, firm yet smooth. Lids lowered over her eyes as she looked at him—strong muscles forming the perfect man. Ari fisted her hand over his shaft, stroking the hard length. Rurik dropped the feather on her chest and instantly drew his hand down to her pussy.

Ari licked her lips and wiggled lower on the bed. Opening her mouth, she angled it toward his cock. Rurik gasped as he got her meaning, but didn't hesitate as he came above her, straddling her head with his thighs. His thick shaft was close to her mouth, and she eagerly drew it to her lips, darting her tongue out over the tip to lightly lick him.

With a small sound of pleasure escaping her, she spread her thighs wide. Rurik latched onto her clit, sucking vigorously as he made love to her with his mouth. His tight body flexed above her, but he was careful not to smother her with his weight as he rocked his hips back and forth, urging her to take the tip more fully into her mouth.

She kissed him gently, twirling her tongue around the ridge, before sucking him deeper. His groans became louder. She pulled back, using her hands to guide him where she wanted him as she nibbled her teeth up and down the sides before latching onto him once more.

Her mind warred with itself, torn between the pleasure of his lips and concentrating on giving as good as she got. He was too large to take comfortably in her mouth, so she used her hands to help stroke the extra length.

Rurik jerked. Ari gasped as he flipped her over, taking her with him as he maneuvered onto his back. The position made it a little easier to breathe and move. He kept her flush to his mouth even as he rocked his hips up toward hers. It was empowering, giving and receiving gratification at the same time.

He grabbed her hips, moving her body against

him. Rurik moaned, softly begging her to stop before he exploded in her mouth. Ari greedily refused to let up, wanting to taste all of him. Her lips rolled faster, sucking harder.

"Ari," he growled, pushing her hips up and away. She fell over to the side, and he was over her before she could catch her breath. His tight body pressed her into the soft mattress.

Spreading her legs, he brought his cock to the apex of her thighs, nudging her open wider with his hips. Rurik closed his eyes and groaned as he thrust forward, burying his cock deep inside her in one confident push. She cried out at the tight fit, the sound joined by his muffled groans.

Rurik smoothed his face between her breasts, massaging both mounds enthusiastically as he began to rock back and forth inside her. He played with her nipples as if fascinated by them, rubbing at the hard peaks only to take them deep into his sucking mouth.

Ari drew her legs up along his sides, allowing for deeper thrusts. It felt good, the way he moved his hips, working them along hers, thrusting within her as he continued to drown her breasts in kisses.

Rurik pulled back, leaning up on his hands as the pace quickened. He kept moving, hooking his arms beneath her legs to pull them over his shoulders. Closing his eyes tight, it was as if he was savoring each stroke of their flesh.

The man definitely knew how to move, and each rhythmic push was punctuated by the graceful flap of his wings as he propelled himself forward.

"Yea, oh, yea," she moaned, arching up into him for more. "Just like that. Yea. Yea!"

Ari tensed, her body building into a climax. He didn't stop thrusting as he reached for the pearl hidden in her slick folds. Her body jerked, tensing on its own accord as she was taken over by the force of her release. Rurik's fingers continued to stimulate her, even as her clit became so sensitive she thought she'd explode if he kept touching her there.

He slowed his pace, and she came down for the briefest of seconds, before he was building her right back up again. It hit her hard, just as good as the first. She tensed, crying out his name in pure ecstasy. "Rurik!"

Suddenly, he grunted, stiffening as he came deep inside her. Ari's body went numb, and her limbs fell to the side. Rurik fell next to her, breathing as heavily as she. Her heart hammered in her chest. Weakly, she wrapped her arms around him, holding him close, liking the feel of his body next to hers. He was safe, and she felt small and protected next to her commander mate.

"I can't feel my body," she whispered.

Rurik chuckled in manly satisfaction, running his hand lightly over her hip. As the back of his fingers glanced near her sex, she jerked in sensitivity. "It feels just fine to me, my queen."

"Mm," she moaned. Even now her body tried to stir him to passion. "Are you going to regret living here at the palace, away from the battlefield?"

"I like the freedom of fighting," he admitted, "but I love you, Ari. Wherever you are, that is my place."

"But what if you come to regret palace life?"

"Then you'll have to make sure it stays interesting." He kissed her shoulder, as he rested his hand against the mound of her sex. Lightly, he wiggled his fingers, tapping them against her slit.

"I'm sure I can come up with something," she teased, mimicking his movements by moving her hand to rest along his inner thigh, right below his shaft. "I know the decision is officially mine, but I'd like to defer the placement of your men to you. I'd like for you to pick your successor."

His eyes met hers and he looked so proud she couldn't help but kiss him.

"Thank you," he said, nodding once.

"There is something I want you to do since we're on the subject of soldiers," Ari said.

"What's that?"

"My cousin. I'd like for her to join the Fifth."

"Her?" Rurik repeated in obvious surprise.

"Vara, my cousin," Ari said.

"A woman in the Fifth? It hasn't been done in a long time."

"So? It's been a while since a pure blood has been on the throne. I think it's time we shook this planet up." Ari smiled.

"When you look at me like that, how can I refuse? It'll be my last standing order with the men. Vara will get her chance, but she'll have to prove herself just like any other soldier."

Ari nodded in pleasure. "Oh, she will. I've seen her fight."

"Now, enough talk of battles, unless you'd like to discuss this soldier right here." Rurik grabbed her hand and slid it up his thigh to his shaft. He kept his hand around hers, moving it up and down over the growing length. It hardened in her hand, and he groaned in satisfaction.

"So many wasted years," she mused. "If only we hadn't been so stubborn. We might have come together sooner."

Rurik rolled onto his back, lifting her so she sat on his stomach. He rubbed her thighs. "Nothing could come of us before. I think fate knew that."

"Why's that? Why would fate deny us the last years?"

"I had to make myself worthy to be your king, and you had to prove to yourself and your people that you could rule. If we had gotten together back then, it would've made these long years harder to bear. Carrying the faint hope that we might someday be was hard enough. If I'd have known you'd be mine, I would have died from the agony of waiting."

She smiled as she leaned over to kiss him. "For a soldier, you've got a most romantic view of things. I like it."

"For a queen, you've got..." He stopped, grinning.

"What?" she laughed. "Can't think of anything?"

"...the most amazing breasts I've ever seen," he

finished, pulling her forward so his face was buried between the large mounds. Taking them in hand, he smothered his face. "Mm, I *murphm memm. I murphm mu oo.*"

Ari laughed, understanding him perfectly. "I love you, too, Rurik. I love you, too."

The End

New York Times & USA TODAY
Bestselling Author

Michelle loves to travel and try new things, whether it's a paranormal investigation of an old Vaudeville Theatre or climbing Mayan temples in Belize. She believes life is an adventure fueled by copious amounts of coffee.

Newly relocated to the American South, Michelle is involved in various film and documentary projects with her talented director husband. She is mom to a fantastic artist. And she's managed by a dog and cat who make sure she's meeting her deadlines.

For the most part she can be found wearing pajama pants and working in her office. There may or may not be dancing. It's all part of the creative process.

Come say hello! Michelle loves talking with readers on social media!

www.MichellePillow.com

facebook.com/AuthorMichellePillow

twitter.com/michellepillow

instagram.com/michellempillow

bookbub.com/authors/michelle-m-pillow

goodreads.com/Michelle_Pillow

amazon.com/author/michellepillow

youtube.com/michellepillow

pinterest.com/michellepillow

Lords of the Var Series
Bestselling Shape-shifter Romance

To play...

Prince Quinn, royal Ambassador, isn't looking for a serious relationship. In fact, he's never even considered it. Hopping from lover to lover, he's content to enjoy himself, never taking anything but his work seriously. However, when Dr. Tori Elliot is sent to the palace to test for biological weapons, he can't seem to stay away from her.

Or not to play...

Tori Elliot has just finished her last assignment and is on her way to a much needed vacation. But when the Human Intelligence Agency stops her ship and demands she heads up a team on some remote planet, she knows it in her best interest not to refuse. Ever serious, she knows she's there to do a job and no matter what, she's going to act like a professional.

Meeting Prince Quinn, his body pressed against another woman in the palace halls, she knows he's not the man for her. Too bad he's the Ambassador and too sexy for his own good. Fighting her desire, Tori must try to do her job while not succumbing to the playful Var prince.

The Playful Prince Excerpt

His sudden movement caught her attention and she realized he stepped toward her. He lifted his hand, as if to touch her. Tori flinched and took a step back.

"Sir," Tori stammered. "I mean, my ... ah?"

"Quinn," he supplied with a rakish smile.

"Yes, my Quinn... wait, no." She took another step back as he moved aggressively forward. The look on his face made her heart flutter in excitement.

"Your Quinn?" he mused in a low tone that sent chills over her spine. "You wish for me to be your Quinn?"

"Stop!" she demanded holding out her hand. He paused in his quest to get to her and grinned, waiting. Tori swallowed, nervous and distracted. "Prince Quinn. I am Dr. Elliot with ESC ... well, actually the HIA, well, not really, technically with HIA or ESC except—"

Was she babbling? Tori was pretty sure it sounded like she was babbling. Scientists didn't babble. It wasn't appropriate. Her scowl deepened. Oh, why was he continuing to look at her like that?

"Well, Dr. Elliot not technically with the HIA or ESC," Quinn said, lowering his jaw as he leaned forward. "I'm H O R N Y and you're extremely pretty."

"H O...? Oh! Really!" Tori gasped, dismayed. She shook her head in disapproval.

"What? You're really so surprised? Can you really blame me, Dr. Elliot? You were staring quite intently at—" Quinn began to motion down, acting as of their conversation was an everyday topic.

Tori held up her hand and shook her head frantically to stop him. Taking a deep breath, she centered her thoughts and made a silent promise to never drink the night before a big assignment again. Surely that is why her heart was pounding so hard and why her limbs were shaking. Swallowing, she forced her voice to rigid calmness. "Is there someone I could talk to about gaining permission to search the cave systems that the biological weapons were discovered in? The HIA has requested that I clear the cave and surrounding area of any and all contamination threats."

Someone other than you, she thought, not caring if he saw her distaste for his lewdness.

Quinn's smile faded and to her surprise, he turned serious. "You think something else is up there?"

"I'm honestly not sure. The recovered weapon appears to be intact and contains enough chemical to wipe out at least five planets. From that bit of information, I would assume there was only the one, unless the caves were being used as a storage unit of some kind, which, given the political climate of your Kingdom, doesn't seem to be the assumption. From what I understand, your father was fighting a war with..."

Tori stopped, realizing that she might be speaking too candidly. That's why she hated being in political situations. Facts were facts and she was use to stating them, regardless of their popularity. In her job facts were all that mattered. In politics, a person was supposed to say things diplomatically, twisting the words into just the right phrase. It was a skill she lacked. She looked up at the Prince. His face hadn't changed. She swallowed nervously. He motioned his hand slightly for her to continue, not looking at all offended by her words.

Weakly, Tori said, "My checking would simply be a wise safety precaution for everyone concerned, especially your people. It won't cost you a thing, if that's your concern. HIA is taking care of my and the other scientists' salary."

Quinn nodded, a motion she hoped was agreement.

"My team has nearly gotten through with the palace inhabitants and so far everyone has tested negative. I believe they're about finished." Tori looked at her clipboard and pretended to scan through the data. This man unnerved her. She couldn't concentrate on what she was saying to him. Was she repeating herself? Was he even listening? Did she tell him yet that they were about done testing the palace inhabitants? She thought it, but did she say it? Damn, he had the most brilliant blue eyes she'd ever seen in her life. Delicately clearing her throat, she said, "But, we'd still like to do a thorough scan of the caves. There is no point in us leaving anything behind."

Quinn seemed to contemplate her words. Tori lowered her voice and stepped closer. He didn't move, except for those blue eyes. They followed her, keeping fixed on her face.

Getting excited, Tori forgot her nervousness as she admitted in a secretive whisper, "There was also something else. I took the liberty of analyzing the strange dark mud on the biological weapon's crate. I believe it's from your marshes, because I found some fresh moss that leads me to believe it wasn't already on the crate when it was brought here. Anyway, there was an extremely high level of what appears to be DTH12 compound, which I'm sure isn't indigenous to this particular planet, being as your swamp soil is classified as GR13H and not TDH14. What doesn't make sense is that DTH12 is primarily found in the slime trail of northeastern yellow slugs on the planet of Fluk in the H ... what? Are you laughing at me?"

Quinn was indeed chuckling. Shaking his head, he said, "Woman, I have no idea what you just said."

Tori frowned. She should have known. Sarcastically, she drawled, "Your mud is neat and I'd like to look at it."

Okay, maybe that was a tad too condescending. Quinn grimaced but didn't appear overly offended. Lucky for her, because he might just be the man she had to impress.

For a complete, up-to-date booklist, visit www. MichellePillow.com

www.ingramcontent.com/pod-product-compliance
Lightning Source LLC
Chambersburg PA
CBHW030413120726
47904CB00007B/2264